The Man Who Knows

An Allegory of Our Time

Humphrey Truman

Truman & Partridge
LONDON. SURBITON

This First Edition
published in 1997

ISBN 0 9531950 0 7

Published by:
Truman & Partridge
PO Box 17600
LONDON WC2N 4AR
England

Printed and Bound in England by:
Williamson Printing Limited
KINGSTON UPON THAMES
Surrey KT1 2SL

Contents

Acknowledgement

The story of *The Man Who Knows* is the basis of a Musical which was first produced on the London Stage at the Tristan Bates Theatre in November 1996.

The music and songs of the Musical were composed by Shaun Purcell, who lives in Ireland near Dublin. The lyrics were written in collaboration between Shaun Purcell and the author.

The songs reproduced in Chapters 6 and 7 of this book, together with the quotations at the head of each chapter, are taken from the musical version of *The Man Who Knows*.

The Man Who Knows

1

Gathering

When all that we hope for is just round the corner *The Seekers*

'GOOD-BYE! I'll call you as soon as I get back.' He didn't know how long he would be away.

Rupert ended his conversation with his office, the last he would have before setting off. He folded the mobile telephone and replaced it in his leather briefcase. As an efficient self-made businessman, it was typical for him to be the first person to arrive at the meeting place, which was in the town park, and not to waste any time when he got there.

He had, of course, left detailed instructions for all his staff explaining unambiguously the tasks that they should carry out. All predictable possibilities were accounted for. In a high tech office like Rupert's, bursting with computers and the latest equipment, nourished by information technology, receiving communications from the world's financial centres throughout each twenty-four hours, it was easy for him to leave behind his own plans for the conduct and management of the business during his short absence.

Rupert stood beside his briefcase, which was bulging with papers in good order, looking at his watch. He was not used to standing around or having to wait for people. Beginning from nothing in business, he had accumulated a lot of money. He had become so used to others complying with his schedule, that the quality of patience was not often called upon by him and he was consequently unpractised in its use.

It was strange that Rupert was setting out on this particular journey. Even a man whom the rest of his community looked upon as possessing everything one could dream of wanting still had his doubts, though this fact was kept hidden and scarcely admitted even to himself. How could he be sure that he had in fact got everything, that there wasn't something else that he was short of, that perhaps other people were receiving advantages he didn't even know about? For the sake of the prosperity of the business and thereby for the benefit of the staff, for whom he felt sincere responsibility, the least he could do, must do, would be to exert himself using all his energies to find out.

'Where on earth is everybody? Is anyone else coming?'

° ° ° ° °

'Hello! I am,' said a young woman.

'Are you another Seeker?' asked Rupert.

'Yes, at least I think so! My name's Helen.'

'What do you mean, you think so?'

Rupert had no time for indecision or uncertainty. You had to come to the point when you spoke to him.

'Well, actually, yes!' said Helen. 'Yes, I have to make the journey.'

'Good, so do I. What do you expect to get out of it?'

'I need to learn,' replied Helen. 'I want to know how to progress. I'm well trained and I've got all the techniques; I just need to know more about the deeper levels.'

Helen was a young career woman well versed in what are currently regarded as modern attitudes to everything. She enjoyed inexhaustible energy; her ambitions lay in treading a path to success at the top within the traditions of the society in which she lived; there was nothing remotely fuddy-duddy about her. She was very competent in all manner of things, in both domestic and working life, which an aspiring young woman needed to contend with. She was not over-powering, as everything she did came naturally and easily to her as it always had done throughout her schooling and upbringing, and all the many courses she had attended. She had always won prizes.

Her over-riding aim was to give herself the best possible chance of accomplishing what she felt she deserved. Therefore she paid constant attention to keeping up a healthy and invigorating life-style. She visited gymnasia, health and fitness clubs on a regular basis, never missing her aerobics classes. She knew all about nutrition and dieting in order to maintain an attractive figure. Her clothes were always fashionable, emphasising her character and personality. Her choice of cosmetics and hairstyle was tasteful instead of flamboyant. At those rare times when she felt less than robustly strong, she treated herself with therapies from alternative medicine which she had studied.

As well as guarding her physical wellbeing, Helen was also concerned with developing the mind and spirit. Reading and theatre-going were essential in order to participate in conversations with her friends. She found that once routines were established in a well-ordered life, it was surprising how much could be fitted in. She managed to find time to attend classes in art and sculpture.

Rupert examined Helen with the usual penetrating look that was customary for him when meeting a stranger for the first time. He was not impressed. He was seldom impressed by anyone nowadays. Why should he be? He knew he had made much more money than most.

An observer of the scene might have thought that Rupert and Helen were two of a kind. They were both ambitious, albeit for different ends. Each was consumed by the objective of an ambition; there was little time left over for consideration and sympathy to another, even a like-minded soul. So they remained apart although they had much in common.

'I want to learn as well,' said Rupert. 'The more information you have the better it is in business.'

Mind you, he already had far more information than he could properly absorb and handle, and certainly far more than anybody else.

o o o o o

As Rupert continued speaking to Helen, a young man approached as if looking for a group. His appearance suggested that his interests were not athletic. His gentle bearing denoted a person of high intelligence who had completed much academic work to become a scholar and researcher of repute. He was an intellectual, an economist. He was Bill Growth.

'Excuse me,' interjected Growth, 'but it's not only information that's important. You have to take into account all the economic theories, the histories of trade and population movements, supply and demand, the application of human resources, the market places.'

Helen was rivetted by such a display of useful knowledge which she had not yet acquired, but which she certainly would one day.

'How fascinating!' she said. 'I'd love to hear more about all your theories. Do they benefit everybody?'

Growth was about to answer, but he was interrupted.

'Well, they've never helped me,' said Rupert. 'Business sense is a sixth sense. If you haven't got it, you won't get on. After all, we all want to be rich, don't we?'

Growth did not come across many men like Rupert in academic life. Thus he was puzzled by such a strain of common sense.

Bill Growth had had a difficult childhood. He had not been happy having been left on his own a great deal, in fact often neglected. There had been no proper supervision of his development, so that he had not had the opportunities of luckier children. During periods of tranquillity he had worked well at school and achieved good results, but inconsistency had not produced the stamina for continuity of effort.

Growth undoubtedly possessed much talent and was widely regarded as a promising young man. Great things were predicted for him in the future; he seemed to have qualities that would enable him to make a fine career. He too felt that he would thrive as an adult, but that was largely because so many people had told him so.

All that, however, was yet to come. For the time being Growth knew that he needed to find consistent guidance and encouragement to help him to apply his talents and avoid being overcome by events. Also there remained a significant difficulty. He was not wholly trusted – which caused him to doubt himself. Were his ambitions impossible to achieve? He had his critics like everyone else. At the moment he needed advice. He needed to find reassurance and confirmation that his chosen path and his attributes would lead to the prizes of fame and prosperity in the future.

No-one should question the integrity of Growth. His aspiration was nothing less than a desire to formulate new economic theories which could be applied in global market places to solve destructive trading problems, releasing energies for the relief of suffering.

o o o o o

Crossing the road into the park was an elderly woman being escorted attentively by a young woman, who had taken her arm to help her across. Not that she needed assistance, for she was in no way frail but full of vigour for her age. During her long life she had always been full of vigour. She had been born into an affluent society; her grounding, education and youthful years were very happy. Since then she had seen much action, she had never been idle. She had witnessed war, earthquakes, floods and famine; she had sailed the seas, crossed deserts and climbed mountains; she had lived in both the Tropics and the Land of the Midnight Sun.

Her name was Molly. More important to her than all this activity, which she hardly rated at all, assuming it to be quite normal for everyone, was her very happy and fulfilled marriage to a handsome kindred spirit. They had produced children who in their turn had become adults with children themselves. Molly's family life was the most valuable of all her wide experiences. As a grandmother, like many others in that respected position, she was now also a widow, grateful to be able to count all the blessings bestowed upon her.

'Thank you so much,' said Molly to her young helper, Debbie. 'Roads always seem to be busy and dangerous. I hope my whole journey won't be like this.'

'Where are you going?' enquired Debbie. 'Is it very far?'

'You're so young you'll probably think I'm mad, but I've heard that there's someone special, a real virtuoso, a Man Who Knows, who can answer all the questions you want to put. I want to know why everything has changed, what's happened to the good old days, why can't we have them back again...

'I heard there's a party going to find this Man Who Knows,' Molly continued, 'and I want to join in. I haven't been travelling for a long while, but all my life when I was younger I loved the thrill of setting off on a journey.'

Debbie became excited by Molly's purpose and intention.

'Of course I don't think you're mad,' she said. 'I'm going to join the party too. That's why I'm around here anyway! When I find him, he's going to help me with my fulfilment, help me to discover myself. It's so exciting; all those anxieties and grievances being carted away for ever!'

° ° ° ° °

Like Molly, Debbie always kept herself active, filling her time usefully, but in different ways with different interests. These interests and concerns would not have bothered the older woman; for the most part she would have been ignorant of them. Debbie always had time to give. Throughout the day from morning to night her innate goodwill made her amiable and cheerful in her workplace. This did not prevent her getting through as much work as, say, Helen. She was always respected; her instant and continual kindness shielded a great strength of character.

Debbie supported various causes of all kinds. She could not ignore an injustice. Therefore after work she devoted her time to attending rallies and taking part in demonstrations. These activities developed into being her hobby, yet it would be foolish and disrespectful to doubt her sincerity and belief that she was playing a small part in bringing about an improved world. She truly believed in trying to love her neighbours, whatever their state of health or circumstances.

Debbie had a loving and generous disposition without envy or malice. She read women's magazines avidly. She knew a great deal about the stars of pop, film, TV soaps and modelling, as well as the stars of astrology. But she was able to keep a balanced perspective. She liked the sun and so far had managed each year a fortnight's holiday in Southern Europe.

She was not a competitive striver or thruster. Her success would come via exercising different qualities. It was most likely that she would eventually be successful in worldly terms and much admired. For the present, she was experiencing worry and uncertainty about herself.

Discovering that they were on the same errand gave Molly and Debbie confidence. They stepped forward more boldly towards the other little group, where Rupert privately continued to make disdainful assessments of his companions.

o o o o o

As the two little parties merged, another man marched up to join them.

'Hello!' he said. 'Is this the group of Seekers?'

'Well, who are you?' asked Rupert, not wishing to be superseded in importance.

'My name's Wilson, but I'm always known as Woody. Have been for years. We must all be friendly, so that's what you should call me.'

Woody Wilson was middle-aged, with a manner and mannerisms conspicuously different from the rest of the group. He had made himself respectable with something of an air of authority about him. But this was not false; it stemmed from the fact that Woody believed in hierarchy – any hierarchy – and he only felt comfortable when he could establish an identifiable place in the order of things, wherever he happened to be. He was not necessarily ambitious to be the top man, but he certainly did not think it appropriate that he should be near the bottom. He regarded himself as vital and important to any society in which he found himself. It was no surprise later on when his new friends learned that he was a town councillor.

Woody was nice enough, inoffensive at heart and he genuinely got on well with people, which was to be a useful characteristic. He didn't bother much with individual thought. His great quality was loyalty. He supported the Monarchy and Parliament; he had served in the Army, being obedient to its traditions; he believed in Law and Order, as he understood them; he attended Council meetings regularly where he could be relied upon by his colleagues; he was loyal to fellow members of any institutions he belonged to. He put his faith in organisations for the structure of society and a proper training for everyone so that they could take up their position within their chosen classification.

It was natural to Woody that he should take charge. The others did not mind, not even Rupert who thought his personal interests would be better served without the responsibility of management.

'Have you all introduced yourselves to each other yet? In my experience, it pays to be well organised; we shouldn't want to set off on a journey as a confused rabble. What a shambles that would be! No, we shall bond together as friends, enjoy each other's company. Travelling can be wearisome without the fun of companionship.'

'How right you are, Woody!' said Molly.

o o o o o

'Can I come too?' said a young boy.

The Seekers looked round in surprise. They were a little put out. Each one had gone to the rendezvous nervously and surreptitiously. Obviously it needs discretion to tell friends that one has heard of the existence of the Man Who Knows and so is going to join a party on a journey to find him. The Seekers were just gaining some confidence. They had looked each other up and down, considered that the potential partners in the enterprise were acceptable – and could have been a lot worse. The comment of the boy was not a welcome jolt. Woody could, however, easily handle the situation and enquired:

'Who are you? What's your name, my friend? Shouldn't you be in school? Does your mother know you're out?'

'My name's Jaz. Look! I've typed it into my computer, J-A-Z. There's no school to-day – half-term holiday. I bet I'd learn a lot if I went with you!'

The youngster, while idly playing and amusing himself in the park, had watched the Seekers gathering themselves together and listened to their conversations without them knowing it. Naturally it would be exciting for him – a chance to join a group of grown-ups on a quest to find a man who could tell him everything he needed to know. That would mean an end to all his adolescent problems, he thought. Apart from the fun of a journey.

Jaz was a teenage schoolboy wanting to be an adult. He was curious about the workings of the world and eager to learn. He was full of vitality but was not unruly; he completed all the schoolwork he was given to do. Of course, he had the undeveloped values of someone his age; nothing else was possible. He mistook things that glitter as being highly esteemed. If he were ever rude, it was not because of an ill nature; he simply hadn't had time to learn to present his language and address tactfully. In truth, his education and progress towards maturity were proceeding satisfactorily, although he thought that sports stars and famous pop stars were the best people to emulate.

'I admire your young spirit, Jaz,' said Woody, 'but really you can't possibly come with us. Another time at a later date perhaps, but you don't have the advanced understanding that we've all got. I'm sorry but – 'No!"

Debbie sensed that the boy was another person whom she could care for; his age didn't matter.

'It would be nice if Jaz could come with us,' she said.

Helen agreed.

'I think he should be able to come too,' she said. 'Surely the Man Who Knows will be able to teach him as much as he learns at school....'

Rupert was impatient with the discussion:

'I really can't see any problems if he joins us. All I want to do is to get going.'

'Well said, Rupert!' added Bill Growth.

Woody knew how to read the reactions emanating from a group discussion:

'All right, that's decided, he can come!'

o o o o o

Nobody else arrived in the park, so the little group assumed that they formed the complete party of Seekers who would journey to find the Man Who Knows. Woody Wilson felt himself to be the natural choice to take charge; the rest didn't think along those lines anyway, so everyone would be happy. Rupert, Helen and Bill Growth appeared to be quite self-contained personalities who would look after themselves. Grandmother Molly and the schoolboy Jaz were also perfectly capable of coping with whatever might happen, but Debbie made a note to be ready to help should any need arise.

Enthusiasm and confidence ran high among them as they anticipated moving off. There was a presumption that they were all looking for the same thing, but this was only true in a general way. It was an illusion.

Each Seeker lived a life confined within his or her own cocoon. Its walls consisted of a unique set of burdens, desires, complications, experiences and wishes. The walls might as well have been physical as it was, apparently, impossible to see out of one's own cocoon into another. At least it was seldom tried. So each lived in a state of isolation, which was camouflaged by the making of pleasurable assumptions about other individuals' circumstances.

Each Seeker had created for himself or herself a concept of the Man Who Knows and assumed that this would be the same concept for everyone else. In fact, they each had a different picture. They thought they were united in their understanding, but they were not. They thought they understood each other, but they did not. They were all isolated from each other, each looking for their own creation, each dwelling in their own imagination, each oblivious to the creations of their companions.

Strangely, it was their isolation which had inspired them to seek the comfort of an infallible source of knowledge. Isolation gave them a unity of purpose.

'We'll all leave together from the Roundabout,' said Woody.

2

The Roundabout

Everyone loves Trivia — *Bill Growth*

OUTSIDE many small towns there is a Roundabout. It is often a local landmark providing roads that lead away into the country as well as the lifeline route back into town. It is a means of communication connecting the town with the wider world beyond. Not all the citizens will want to venture out.

Coming from different backgrounds with different outlooks on life, the Seekers met at the Roundabout, the best focal point from which to set off on their journey to find the Man Who Knows. Individually, they had prepared themselves for the journey. Each person had justified in his or her own mind that this was a profound course of action to be taking. What else could be done if one nursed uplifting ambitions? Doubt did not exist, did not occur; thoughts better left unspoken soon will not trouble the conscience. After all, who could say positively at this stage whether or not their confident aspirations might have been misconceived?

Nerves were quickly overcome. Hindrances were surmounted, preventing them becoming insuperable barriers. The activity of preparation, once begun, created its own energy, which in turn created optimism. Apprehension was replaced by enthusiasm and determination, with a growing conviction that the course of action proposed must inevitably lead to desirable solutions to perplexities.

Comradeship strengthened their resolve. Unity of purpose provides great fun, whatever the objective; it is important to incorporate fun into an enterprise. It became easy for the Seekers to escape and leave behind the old state of mind, characterised by uncertainties, confusions, misconceptions, improbabilities masquerading as possibilities, absence of purpose or aim and other oppressions.

'Are we all here?' said Woody. 'Good to see that everybody's ready!'

'Yes, we're definitely on the right path, doing the right thing,' replied Debbie, remembering her experience of many marches and demonstrations.

'It's certainly to our credit that we have fathomed it out for ourselves,' said Growth.

Molly had as much vitality as any of them. 'I know I shall love it all,' she said. 'Starting off is thrilling!'

Helen came straight to the point: 'Let's move quickly!'

A problem soon arose requiring immediate decision, namely, which was the right road for them to take? The Roundabout offered a number of possible directions.

o o o o o

Happily the Keeper of the Roundabout was always available to give advice. The Keeper, named Trivia, was as charming a young lady as you will ever meet. From her home nearby, she had helped many travellers. At least she believed she had – so usually did they.

Trivia was delightful. She was tidy, well dressed, clean, well washed, as bright as a button. She was always agreeable, cheerful and ready with a natural smile. She presented both herself and her ideas attractively. She was neither very, very good nor very bad. She was never in too much of a hurry. It was effortless to pass the time of day with her, an event that would be remembered with pleasure.

If the picture is to be complete, however, one must recognise that her pleasing character did have a few drawbacks. She was experienced in her ways, but not mature. Years of pleasantries had made her somewhat superficial, but they had also made her clever in her habits. She could bend your will to follow her whim and you would enjoy the process. She would willingly help you – to follow her own ideas. She appeared to have others' best interests at heart.

Trivia could always occupy your time and your attention, and very pleasant it would be. She would distract you from your original intentions, while simultaneously leaving you feeling happy about the change, thinking that you had made a wise decision. If you wanted to tackle a project that might be baffling or laborious, she could create endless diversions by thinking up plausible alternatives, all of which would be enjoyable.

How cruel it is to mention that such a popular and enchanting a person as Trivia could possibly lack a couple of attributes that would have been welcome. She was not good at presenting wisdom, nor, among the many blessings she possessed, could she count on determination.

These deficiencies were unfortunate, since the Seekers wished to consult Trivia to take her advice. The contrast between their own eagerness and her laid back approach was striking. It was the growing confidence of the Seekers that had enabled them to begin their quest in the first place. Their collective drive would overcome Trivia's superficiality, though only after they had paused to indulge in such delightful company. Then truer reflections would guide them to continue towards the answers they were seeking.

o o o o o

Sitting on a grass bank in the sunshine, leaning against the fence outside Trivia's little house, was a young man named Snow.

He was amusing himself by idly playing some tunes on a violin, which he always carried with him, while waiting for Trivia to emerge. Snow was a cheerful young fellow, very quiet and thoughtful, who never imposed forthright views on other people. But he was not passive; there was a strength of personality emanating from his demeanour. He was well educated and cultured, having received much good fortune, which he shared as best he could by finding time for everybody.

In their quandary as to which route to take and while needing to find Trivia, the Seekers approached Snow.

'That's a lovely sound,' said Debbie. 'What is it that you are playing?'

'Nothing in particular. Just passing the time while I wait for Trivia to come out.'

'Maybe you'd like to pass the time by telling us how to find the way to the Man Who Knows?' said Woody, forcefully.

'Who's he, for goodness sake?' Snow was obviously surprised by the question.

'You don't know about him?' asked Debbie. 'He's the one who's meant to know all the answers. He'll sort things out for all of us.'

'He sounds like a useful fellow to know. I've never even heard of him. Is there really such a person?'

Debbie responded with assurance: 'Sure, there certainly is, and we're going to find him. Each one of us has questions which he will be able to answer. It's going to be so beautiful.'

'Nowadays, one suffers so much from uncertainty,' said Growth, convincingly. 'All is supposed to be explained and predictable, but nothing turns out as it's meant to be. Advice is ambiguous and contradictory. The Man Who Knows offers the voice of authentic authority.'

With his kindly nature, Snow wanted to give them any help he could:

'You seem to want to find this fellow pretty badly. You'll have to ask Trivia. This is where she lives. She'll be out in a minute.'

After hearing the voices in conversation, Trivia came out of her house and garden to see the party of Seekers and her friend Snow, whom she greeted warmly with a cheery 'Hello, Snow!'

Her sunny disposition and friendly behaviour encouraged them to want to know her. It was Woody who spoke first.

'Hello!' he said. 'I wonder if you can help us? Sorry to bother you.'

'Oh, you're not bothering me! I suppose you're all on a journey and want my advice. People always seem to ask me things! It's all right, that's what I'm here for. Where are you all going?'

'It's probably a bit unusual,' said Woody, 'but we don't know where we're going! We're trying to find the way to the Man Who Knows. Do you happen to know him?'

'I can't say that I do! Never heard of him. Something new at last! Well, there are two main roads leading off from this Roundabout. I catch all the chatter and gossip from the travellers and, from what I hear, they usually take one of these. Perhaps your friend lives at the end of one of them?'

'What are these two roads?' asked Helen.

'There's the Road of Reality,' said Trivia, 'and then there's the Road of Imagination.'

Helen was impressed: 'Wow, the Road of Reality! That sounds just the job. Interesting! What can you tell us about that one?'

Trivia leaned against her garden fence to describe it to them.

° ° ° ° °

'The Road of Reality...,' she began. 'Travellers normally set off in a state of enthusiasm, but the path seems to lead downwards. It passes between bushes and hedges on either side which are too tall to see over. The sky is grey and menacingly cloudy; there will be storms. You see shadows and hear voices, you sense presences which are disturbing. Round every bend lies the expectation of something sinister. One has to brace oneself and summon an effort of will before turning a corner to face a new aspect. And there are a lot of corners. Nothing can be taken for granted. The unending, unpredictable surprises become exhausting. This road is extremely tiring after a while...

'Voices shout out: 'You can't do that!' 'Wait!' 'Not this way!' 'No!' 'Wrong again!' Sometimes there is temporary encouragement. But you don't get time to enjoy it before the next setback occurs, which is bound to be of a different kind. You will pass many strangers, all pretending to demonstrate a self-assurance which they do not actually feel. The great thing is to remember to keep moving on. No-one will have much time to give you...

'Later on, another major road leads off at a junction. That is the Road of Science. Quite a few people transfer to it thinking it will answer their needs more precisely. But frankly, the travellers on both these roads seem to me to finish up introverted. Their introspection is sad. I don't recognise happiness in their faces.'

Molly was horrified: 'I don't like the sound of that at all. It's not what I'm looking for!'

Helen's opinion was different: 'This road needs a lot of decisions. That would suit me fine.'

'A lot of people aren't properly trained,' explained Rupert, 'so they're bound to make a mess of it - you've got to expect that. The trouble is, they don't understand the principles of being in a competitive business. Once they've found the basic guiding philosophy, like I had to, then they ought to be able to cope with the inevitable ups and downs that arise.'

Molly was not satisfied and asked Trivia: 'Please could you tell us about the other one? Is the Road of Imagination any better?'

Trivia sat on the grass with Debbie and Molly.

'It depends what you like...,' she said.

o o o o o

'From the stories I hear, the Road of Imagination is a very different type of road: The scenery you pass is simply whatever you want it to be. Your favourite flowers by the roadside, valleys dropping away to provide glorious views, grass slopes with a variety of green leafed trees and shrubs, hedges for butterflies, distant snow-covered mountains glistening in the sunshine beneath rich blue skies...

'On the edge of the sky are huge fluffy clouds of the purest white, from whence spring spectacular rainbows. Rain falls continuously from the clouds, but never where you happen to be, always on distant places, places you have passed and places you will come to shortly. You never get wet yourself...

'One doesn't meet strangers, so neither your patience nor impatience is tested. Every single fancy and temptation will be indulged; every plan conceived will be finished successfully. As talents and virtues become required along the way, you will find you possess them abundantly...

'The road doesn't lead anywhere; you wouldn't want it to! It's such tremendous fun, just being on this road, that you want the journey to go on and on and on. But, to be honest, I sometimes wonder if the travellers on this road are always telling me the truth? I hope I haven't got a suspicious mind?'

'Of course not,' said Molly. 'I'm sure you haven't. It's splendid! Splendid! The Road of Imagination is definitely the one for me.'

'I'm afraid I don't agree,' argued Rupert. 'Do you really believe what you've just heard? Reality may sound gruesome, but at least you know what you're getting. By any standards it must be absolutely essential that we take the Road of Reality.'

Helen was quick to support the argument: 'Yes, Rupert's right. Who's to say that imagination's always good? Haven't you ever had a nightmare?'

'But that's such a narrow-minded view,' said Debbie. 'The very essence of human existence depends upon our expanding vision. It's only through dreaming that we can be exactly who we want to be.'

'And it's only in the abstract that all my theories can be worked out,' added Growth.

'I don't care much for imagination myself,' Woody admitted, rather sheepishly. 'It's never seemed to work for me. I like to keep my feet on the ground – it's safer that way!'

The Seekers seemed to have stumbled upon differences of opinion which could not be reconciled. Which road should they follow? Woody assumed control and suggested a democratic vote. Jaz wanted to be included but this was arbitrarily forbidden by Woody, on the grounds that Jaz was too young and immature to have a worthwhile view.

A vote was taken by a show of hands, which resulted in a tie. Molly, Debbie and Growth chose the Road of Imagination; Helen, Rupert and Woody preferred the Road of Reality.

Trivia spotted the impasse and it was through her tact and ability to please everyone that the dilemma was eased. She pointed out how difficult it was to make a choice. Sometimes it was unfair to be expected to do so, and even she occasionally made a decision but ended up changing her mind. It was not always the best thing to get your own way. Not all the Seekers agreed with her thinking, but they were all captivated by her charm.

Trivia next informed them that there was a third road, a small one, leading off the Roundabout. She had not mentioned it before because it was almost never used. She had not heard travellers talk about it, so she called it the 'Unknown Road', which it was to her.

'Where is it?' said Helen, 'I can't see another road...'

'It's over there, through a gate,' answered Trivia.

'Excuse me,' said Snow politely, 'but as you hold divided opinions and you're enterprising people, why don't you try the Unknown Road? Trivia and I will show you where it is.'

This suggestion, which would settle the dispute, was accepted without a murmur; the whole group moved off towards the Gate.

3

At the Gate

No-one can know
what sort of adventure we might discover — *Rupert*

THE SEEKERS crossed one of the major roads from the Roundabout and walked a short way down an almost hidden lane. They came to a very large old gate situated between high ill-kept hedgerows that grew to protect the fields on either side. The Gate constituted a considerable obstacle; it had to be opened, as some of the Seekers would be unable to climb over. There appeared to be no mechanism for opening it.

A large five-barred gate was a challenge to Jaz, who felt impelled to climb to the top. He sat astride the top and looked around him. He saw a footpath, overgrown through under-use, leading away from the Gate on the far side.

Then he shouted out: 'Look, this must be it! I can see a signpost.'

'Well, can you read it?' asked Woody.

'It says, 'The Road to Knowhere',' reported Jaz.

'I think he's got it!' said Growth.

'He must be right, you know,' confirmed Rupert.

'Where else could the Man Who Knows live but in Knowhere?'

The Seekers pushed and examined the Gate to see how it might be opened. Only Trivia was not surprised at the problem. She knew that it had not been used for years. Snow suggested that one or two of the party should climb over, to see if it might be easier to open from the other side. Jaz leapt off the top and tumbled to the ground, to be joined by Helen whose gymnastic training enabled her to clamber over the obstacle. Reaching the ground, Helen inspected the gate posts. On one were large, rusty hinges; on the other she discovered an old, creaking, country-style latch. When she applied sufficient pressure, the latch moved; she announced triumphantly that she could pull the gate open from where she was on the far side. Molly thought it very odd, that when you're already on the other side, then you can open it easily! To Woody, such an arrangement represented bad organisation, which he had no sympathy with – he became flustered momentarily:

'It's crazy!' he exclaimed. 'There's no organisation! You can't open a gate till you've passed through it!'

As the Seekers eagerly passed through the open gateway, Rupert admonished Woody:

'Don't worry about that now. The important thing is that we've found the Road to Knowhere and can begin our journey at last.'

They were longing to leave. The Seekers took their first footsteps along the pathway shown by the signpost, but forgot to shut the gate. Snow thoughtfully moved forward to close it, calling out as he waved them off:

'Goodbye to you all, and good luck!'

Debbie turned round, astonished:

'Hey, aren't you going to come along with us? I'd love to hear more of your music – that'll keep us in good spirits on the way.'

'Well, what a kind invitation! I suppose I've got enough spare time; I confess you've made me curious to meet this special person. It's new to me, it all seems fun, so if I could and nobody minds, I'd like to come.'

'That's great! And Trivia, you must come too.'

'Please do,' pleaded Growth.

'That'll be nice for us,' added Molly.

'I'm sure we'd all like that,' said Woody, anxious to maintain his leading position by confirming what seemed to be agreed already among his friends.

'Oh yes, thank you,' said Trivia. 'Thank you! I really want the chance to come. I've heard so much about the other roads, but nothing about this one. It never gets mentioned. I'd just love to know what it's like and where it goes. Come on Snow!'

Snow guided Trivia through the gateway to join the group. They shut the gate, put the latch back in its place and all started off together.

The Seekers were delighted to be joined by the extra travellers added to the party. A larger number was likely to be more entertaining.

The Seekers discussed the newcomers amongst themselves. It always takes some time before outsiders are fully accepted on equal terms.

'What a splendid creature Trivia is!' said Growth softly. 'I'm not falling in love with her, but I wouldn't mind spending some time in her company!'

'There are not many young women around who are so endlessly endearing with such a variety of subjects to be interested in.' Woody's comment was slightly patronising, though it was intended to offer some encouragement to Growth.

'Yes, I am fascinated by the variety of her ideas,' said Debbie. 'You could never be bored in her company.'

'Now hang on!' said Helen. 'I like Trivia too and I'm glad she's coming with us. But jumping about like that on the surface of everything can't be enriching or fulfilling. You've got to make a selection, decide what you're going to do then give it all the attention you can. Let's concentrate on our journey!' Helen was down to earth.

'We shouldn't waste time thinking about things that don't matter,' said Rupert. 'We've decided to go. Let's push on to find the Man Who Knows.'

Molly could see it would be useful if she acted as peacemaker if the younger people looked like having disagreements.

'Trivia is a very important person – although something of a conundrum! – and she always will be,' she said. 'She's not likely to move her home and any of us could come back in the future to make friends with her. The trouble is that by then we'll all know everything, so it won't be the same as it is now.'

As they progressed along the way and they came to know each other better, their companionship became more cordial and affectionate. They learned of the virtues that each of them possessed and paid each other compliments.

'Everyone loves Trivia!' said Growth, with an eye to the future.

Elated by this remark, and thinking it to be true, Trivia picked some flowers and gave him a bunch of forget-me-nots. It was a nice gesture.

4

On the Journey

Does love whisper, does it sing *Debbie*

THE TRAVELLERS now consisted of the Seekers together with Jaz, Trivia and Snow. They continued their journey to Knowhere, following the signposts along the Unknown Road. It was clear that the pathway was seldom used; being untrodden, the grass and weeds had grown tall and in places there was thick undergrowth stretching across the path. But there was no serious hardship. They walked along, chatting agreeably, conversations and laughter prevailing as they changed companions in little knots of twos and threes. The countryside they passed through comprised a mixture of fields and hedges, or woods and copses. Luckily the weather was perfect for their needs, being warm and sunny. At intervals they would stop to refresh themselves and take a cooling drink.

'What a lovely day's walk!' said Molly. 'Shall we rest for a while?' She was not tired, being as strong as any of them. She knew that an integral part of the enjoyment of a good walk was to take a rest now and again.

'Yes, that's a good idea,' agreed Debbie. 'This is a nice spot, let's stop here!'

When they were lounging on the ground in relaxation, she went on, 'Come on Snow, play for us!'

Snow was hesitant, not wanting to impose the sound of music on anyone who sought silence, or preferred to listen for birdsong; nor did he wish to intrude upon anyone who wanted to be alone with their own thoughts.

'All right, as long as that's what everybody wants, I'll be happy to play. What about this?'

Snow played a jolly little tune that began softly and slowly. As it became more vibrant, suitable for dancing, Debbie and Trivia stood up to dance. Jaz was intrigued and so the two young women incorporated him into their dance.

The others looked on while idly chatting. The music and dancing finished as the conversation continued.

'I'm glad we chose the Unknown Road,' said Growth. 'Funny we haven't seen a single stranger when it's so pleasant.'

'What do you expect?' said Rupert. 'Trivia advised us it was virtually unused. But I admit it's surprising we haven't seen anyone coming towards us. It is a bit of a one-way street.' Rupert didn't usually admit anything.

Helen knew the answer: 'Of course, it's obvious! Once you've met the Man Who Knows, it's clear that you don't need to come back.'

'What's the point of a return journey,' asked Rupert, 'when you've learned everything you need to know?'

'It's a good thing that we're all together,' said Growth. 'It's a nice road, but I wouldn't want to be travelling on it alone.'

'It's best to do anything in a group – a well organised group, of course,' observed Woody.

'But why is it so essential to be in a group here on this road?' asked Rupert. 'What are you worried about? It's not dangerous.'

'Well, so we've found out,' Growth commented, 'but we didn't know that before we started.'

Woody did not enjoy discussions he considered too clever; they made him feel uncomfortable.

'Anyway,' he said, 'we won't get far waiting here. Let's move on.'

Snow had been listening while he toyed with his violin. He began to strum a few notes.

'Let's not be in a rush,' said Debbie. 'We can all have a dance before we go.'

Snow produced from his repertoire another engaging tune, but this one had a rhythmic vigour. It was impossible not to react to the beat, so before long the whole party was dancing - even Woody. Molly showed a lilting style alongside the jiving of the younger set.

Woody began to feel foolish, coughed pointedly and brought the dance to an end.

'Right, very enjoyable,' he said, without much sincerity. 'Right, let's be on our way!'

While the party pulled themselves together to continue the walk, Jaz, who was ready first, ran on ahead. Abruptly he stopped, gazed into the distance, then turned round and shouted back:

'Look, I can see something in the distance! It looks like an Archway. Do you think that's it?'

'That must be Knowhere!' said Snow.

5

Meeting the Man Who Knows

History talks and music speaks,
murmurs in the mind — *The Man Who Knows*

THE ARCHWAY lay at the end of the Unknown Road. It was the entrance to Knowhere, the home of the Man Who Knows. The Seekers' party passed through the arch and followed the signs which pointed to the centre of the town. Having completed their journey safely, they were in a euphoric mood. They felt fit and ready to begin the meeting they had come for as soon as possible.

Near the middle of the town was a green and it was here that they first saw the Man Who Knows. He was sitting in the sunshine on a large type of chair, not a throne, but a wooden chair with a high back and arm rests. He was reading some documents. On a table beside him were several books. He was dressed in a gown reminiscent of the robes worn by a university chancellor. In his case, they were not overly splendid, but were nevertheless distinctive and distinguished.

The Seekers were surprised that they felt no sense of being overawed in the presence of one upon whom they had invested such greatness in their minds. The characteristics revealed, both by the expression on his face and by his bearing and body language, were friendliness, bonhomie, humility and an easy assurance stemming from a modest confidence in his own considerable abilities.

The Man Who Knows rose to greet them.

'Welcome to Knowhere, my friends! I always enjoy meeting new arrivals – I wish I could do it more often. I hope you had a good journey, without any accidents or bad experiences.'

The whole party excitedly offered their hellos and greetings; Molly in particular said what a marvellous time she had had on the journey. Rupert was not at all elated, merely observing that they had not seen a single other person on the way.

'That is no surprise!' said the Man Who Knows. 'My friends, I commend you for tackling the Unknown Road and for coming to see me. My colleagues and I are always waiting to help people, but too often they don't come and ask, even when they know that they ought to. Many people think they can muddle along happily through life by themselves. What a mess!'

Growth was startled by the Man Who Knows' reference to his colleagues.

'Do you mean to say there are lots of you?' he enquired. 'Are you all Men Who Know?'

'Oh yes!' said the Man Who Knows. 'There have to be others in my position There are so many questions to be answered that I couldn't possibly do it all alone. In fact, I sometimes need to refer to other specialists myself!'

Woody noticed the signs of a man with responsibilities and authority, and sensed some fellow feelings.

'Well now, look here,' he said, 'I'm sure we needn't take up much of your time; I expect you're pretty busy. I have some experience of these matters and know what it's like.'

Nevertheless Woody was ignored.

'Let's sit down for some serious business,' said the Man Who Knows. 'Collect your thoughts together and let me know the questions you've brought to me.'

The Man Who Knows sat in his chair, as befits a man past seventy, while the Seekers sat on the ground around him. Snow asked politely if he and Trivia could be excused the session as they had only accompanied the group as extras. They wanted to explore Knowhere, which Trivia found enchanting, and had brought no worries to bother him about.

'Very well, my friends, of course. Nothing will be forced on you in this place.'

'Do you really know everything?' asked Jaz. Helen rebuked him, saying that it was rude to ask a question like that, casting doubt about the capability of the Man Who Knows. She then suffered a rebuke in her turn.

'Oh no!' said the Man Who Knows. 'No, all it means is that this young man hasn't had time yet to acquire experience, to school himself for the time ahead.'

Turning to Jaz, he went on: 'Well now, my young friend, seeing that you have some doubts, you want to find out if I really know everything, you go first and tell me what you want. First of all, tell me your name?'

Jaz replied, giving his name, but after that he felt embarrassed at being put on the spot. The rest of his answer was in the manner of thinking out loud. He wanted to be a star footballer scoring goals. What about being a racing driver – the thrill of speed? Obviously it would help to be clever: to save a lot of bother at school; and with grown-ups; to know all about Shakespeare. To have everything you wanted needed a lot of money – he must be rich. Lastly, having a good nature, he wanted to help his family and make them proud. While voicing these reflections, Jaz became shy, realising that he didn't know what was best.

'Thank you, Jaz,' said the Man Who Knows in a kindly, avuncular manner. 'You won't have much to worry about when you can express the depth of your thoughts so lucidly. Now, let me deal with the real problems. I'll take them one at a time.'

'But when will I be a grown-up?' insisted Jaz. 'What will I do? Will I be famous? Can't you tell me?'

'I think I've answered you already, Jaz. We must keep moving on. Now you, my friend,' he said, turning to Helen.

'I really must have a much higher status,' replied Helen, 'a more respected position in society. Through my own efforts I've achieved a lot so far, but now I'm on the springboard ready for something new. I'm not sure what it is or how to get there quickly. I sense a new understanding would translate my chances into something bigger.'

'It will require a great deal of thought and effort. You'll need a lot of extremely hard work.'

'But I'm doing that already!'

'That's fine, wonderful! If I were in your shoes, I'd be more than happy. Just carry on as you are – you're doing well. I'm sure something will come of it eventually – and perhaps even sooner than that!'

A frown crossed Helen's face momentarily.

It was Rupert's turn next.

'I'm in business,' he said. 'My parents were poor, but I have made millions. I need to go on making profits because in any society it's better that the creators of wealth should have decent opportunities. Basically, how can I maximise profitability, harness the latest technologies to the control of costs? I need to be able to predict the social trends in our world so that I can let my staff prepare detailed projections for the next twenty-five years.'

'You're making things harder for yourself. When you've assessed the movement of market forces in a geo-political framework, then it's easy!'

'Which fields will be the best investments for the next hundred years?' persisted Rupert.

But the Man Who Knows had dealt with Rupert's question and he now pointed at Bill Growth.

'How can I develop my own economic theory,' said Growth, 'one that can really make a change for the good of all? The economic theory of Growth? I want plans that will iron out the problems of international trade and the pricing of resources.'

'What a splendid idea, a great ambition! There are many paths up to the summit – everybody follows a different one. Let me hear more!'

'My comprehensive theory,' continued Growth, 'will embrace social, environmental and cultural issues.'

'Ah yes, I know the answer you want – and it will be available soon! Advanced concepts and plans are being developed, even as we speak!'

Although Molly was the oldest of the Seekers, with her energy and enthusiasm she could hardly wait for her chance to speak, so she butted in:

'Please, please, no more changes, please! In my time I've seen almost everything change. When will it all end, what's the purpose of it all? Such happy times when I was young, but what will happen to my grandchildren? What am I passing on to them? Will they be able to cope? That's what I want to know, and it worries me stiff.'

'You must be comforted that so many people share those thoughts,' replied the Man Who Knows, 'so that you are not alone. It would be a terrible burden to contemplate on your own. So don't make the mistake many others make by thinking you are set apart. I think I can see that you will treat your concerns in a mature way. That's the most important thing. That you can cope with the situation and not let it get you down!'

The kind-hearted Debbie was patient and never thought or needed to push in. She waited till almost the end before making her plea to the Man Who Knows:

'In order to help me in all the things I want to do, first I must understand myself. I want my real, true character to be fulfilled, I want to find myself. Unless I know who I am, what I am here for, it is difficult to join the right campaigns against all the pain and sorrow that I see.'

'Firstly, you should make up your mind,' replied the Man Who Knows. 'Do you want to look for your inward virtues and limitations, or for your outward characteristics? Are you supposing that all these things are compatible? From my point of view, of course, I also have to consider many other factors. Although your understanding is not complete, you do very well to tackle these issues, to play a part that will benefit your community.'

Debbie did not think the answer to her question was very satisfying, but her good nature did not allow her to show any ill feeling, nor to press ahead with a further enquiry.

Only Woody of the Seekers had not yet participated in the discussion, and now he rose and stepped forward to be close to the Man Who Knows.

'I've waited till last,' he said, 'thoroughly enjoyed listening to your explanations and hearing you talk. It gives me so much pleasure to meet you and be in your company at last. Could I become a Man Who Knows myself? I expect you and I are similar in temperament - although you are much more senior to me, of course. Who should I apply to? Presumably there's a selection board and then a training programme?'

'Well, you have conceived an admirable ambition!' concluded the Man Who Knows. 'What would your friends think of that? *(In fact, they were all laughing at Woody behind his back!)* The calling I share with my brothers is both honourable and necessary. Citizens demand our services – there's plenty of work to be done. I wish you the best of luck – if you can make the grade!'

The seminar reached its ending at the same time as Snow and Trivia returned to the green to rejoin the group. The Man Who Knows, as dignified and polite as his fine manners prescribed, rose from his chair to greet them.

'Let me welcome back the explorers,' he said good-humouredly. 'Come and join us again! What did you think of Knowhere? Was it what you expected?'

'I loved all the flowers,' said Trivia, 'all those gorgeous colours and so many of them. I've never seen so many in one place before.'

'It's a fine place to see, Sir!' said Snow. 'I thought that the atmosphere was wholesome and refreshing; the people seem to have assurance as they quietly go about their errands. This poise and easy confidence was the feature that made its mark on me.'

'Well, I suppose that if they all know what they're doing, they can afford to be confident,' commented Trivia. 'I noticed too that there seemed to be no uncertainty about the place.'

The Man Who Knows spent a few minutes chatting and exchanging views privately with Trivia. It was unexpected and surprising to see them getting on so well together. Meanwhile, Snow began to talk to the Seekers. They had all risen to their feet and were muttering among themselves.

'How have you been getting on?' asked Snow. 'After the efforts you made to get here, has it all been worth-while? Is everybody's mind at rest and contented?'

There was some hesitation for a moment before Growth answered: 'Frankly, so far, it hasn't been quite as rewarding as we wanted. But this was only a first meeting, and there will be more to come. No doubt everything will become clear later on.'

The Seekers were still optimistic as Helen raised a good point:

'The obvious question that springs to mind is – how, when and where the Man Who Knows acquired all this superior knowledge he's supposed to have?'

'Well, why don't you ask him?' said Snow. 'Don't be afraid, you won't catch him out! Surely he's been trained to handle difficulties that would trip up an ordinary mortal.'

The Man Who Knows finished talking to Trivia and, while moving towards the main group, he overheard their conversation.

'Oh dear!' he said. 'My friends, you are absolutely right to ask about anything at all that's bothering you. How right you are! I think you've been listening to me and learning already – and we've only just met! So think what you'll be like when we've finished!'

'Let me tell you how lucky you are at this time,' he went on. 'Once a year my fellows and colleagues and I all meet for our conference, a Conference of all the Men Who Know. We have to keep our professional knowledge and abilities up to date in the same way as ordinary citizens do. We couldn't do our job otherwise. The timing is perfect – we meet next week.'

'Couldn't we come,' asked Helen, 'to see for ourselves how you are all trained and where you learn it all?'

'Rather like going back to original sources,' added Growth.

'Oh no!' said the Man Who Knows. 'It's private and highly confidential. Definitely not possible! However, I'll tell you what I'll do. If you choose to nominate two persons, I'll arrange for them to be allowed in – as a privilege. I don't want you to think there are any secrets to be hidden.'

'I'll go!' said Rupert, as if no other decision was possible.

Woody coughed, straightened his tie and said: 'I would be prepared to represent us if someone would like to come with me.'

'What about me? I could do that,' shouted Jaz.

'Perhaps as the only grandparent present,' said Molly, 'I should decide, to spare the chance of anyone feeling hurt. Let Snow and Trivia go – they are impartial as they did not come here like the rest of us 'on business', so to speak, but they came only as observers.'

'They can come back and tell us all about it,' said Growth.

Molly's idea seemed to be the best solution and everyone agreed.

The Man Who Knows addressed the two who were chosen to attend and witness the Conference:

'Mr Snow and Miss Trivia, you will be very welcome to come and see us all in action, to see us under instruction, so that you can learn how it's done. Meet me at the beginning of next week and I'll take you along!'

6

The Conference of the Men Who Know

We learn from each other
and we teach one another *The Men Who Know*

THE CONFERENCE of the Men Who Know was customarily attended by all the qualified Men Who Know from far and wide, from countries and cultures spread across the world. It took place annually in the town of Knowhere. The many different events making up the Conference were arranged in the Great Hall, smaller halls, lecture rooms, libraries, galleries, laboratories and in fitness and recreational facilities. It was the biggest event of each year in the town.

The procedures of the first morning were those usually followed at any conference or business convention. There was registration for all those Men Who Know who had received proper accreditation in advance, at which each one was given the programme of events for the week. This was immediately followed by the opening ceremony in the Great Hall, where all the participants came together for the first time. It was an impressive sight. All the Men were wearing either robes or academic gowns. Except for one. There was one

Man Who Knows who came from Off Shore who wore short beach trousers, a brightly coloured Hawaiian sports shirt and sandals.

It was a huge privilege for Snow and Trivia to be allowed to attend. They looked comfortable and relaxed in casual day dress, curious to see the exciting activities that were in store.

The Conference and its programme were arranged by Jane Hyper-Byte, an intellectual of exceptionally high intelligence. An energetic and vivacious young woman, she carried the burden easily and competently of acting as the Conference secretary, registrar, organiser, programme co-ordinator and information officer. There was no need for publicity or public relations, all the events being strictly private.

Jane Hyper-Byte began the opening ceremony with a short talk describing the purpose and objectives of the Conference:

'As we begin another of our annual Conferences, I thank you all for coming to attend so enthusiastically. Under Paragraph 2 of the Third Appendix to Schedule Number 5 of Part 4 of our Charter, this Conference has been planned in order that all the participants may be made aware of and conversant with the most modern developments affecting our calling. I have planned lectures on all subjects in which we must be able to profess expert knowledge. Therefore there will be lectures on: philosophy, economics and monetarism, environmental studies, computer and information technologies, meditation and self-hypnosis, visual arts, particle physics, anthropology, molecular biology, inter-personal communication skills, stress tension and depression, human resources, massage therapies and weight training, comparative religion, science fiction and futurology. And others....

'I welcome you here, and recommend that you attend all of these, leaving time of course for personal study and self-improvement. Discussions of the subjects will take place in small groups.'

Before leaving the Great Hall, the Men Who Know enjoyed singing a favourite song to unite and inspire them in their efforts. As they heard the sound of the organ, they all stood up:

'We are held in awe,
Respected and esteemed, complimented, worshipped and revered,
We give confidence and comfort, guidance and advice,
But most of all
We know everything that you need to know.

'Remember, we were here first, and I know you will agree,
You cannot do without us, you taught us we must be.
The more that we tell them, the greater their dismay,
The greater their confusion, the more we have to say.

'As the Men Who Know, we can point the way,
Save you the struggle and the strife.
With a deep understanding, patient and true,
We will lead you through the maze of life.'

The Men Who Know left the Great Hall after the opening meeting ended and dispersed to go to different venues for instruction in the various subjects. Snow and Trivia went out into the street as well. Trivia was bewildered by what she had just heard – it was far outside her experience.

'Have they really got to know all that?' she asked Snow. 'It would be too much for me.'

'Of course it would, silly!' replied Snow. 'These men are trained to do their job.'

During the period of the Conference, Snow and Trivia were free to wander about the town visiting and observing the experts at work. It was all very friendly. Sometimes they were accompanied by their own Man Who Knows, the one who had invited them, but at other times they turned to the nearest person to put their queries.

Snow carried a clipboard to which he pinned a copy of each day's programme of events. They chose to see as wide a variety of activities as they could, so that they would be able to report to the Seekers as fully as possible. Interesting incidents succeeded one another day by day.

o o o o o

In one spacious hall there was no furniture at all, just a large floor area. Trivia thought it looked like a dance hall, but it turned out to be the Department of Economics. There were several Men Who Know standing in the middle of the hall, each occupying a small territory of his own. They were all juggling.

'Who are they?' asked Snow. 'Whatever are they doing that for?'

'Those people are our economic experts,' replied the Man Who Knows. 'They're checking their research. They always have to juggle with facts and figures. Oh dear! There goes inflation!' he said, as one of the jugglers dropped a ball. 'Now you watch, he'll throw interest rates higher to give himself more time.'

Two of the experts began conversing excitedly:

'I think I've got it!' said the first expert.

'That's great! Now we can put our research together to produce an agreed hypothesis,' replied the second.

They began to juggle between themselves, passing the objects they were using to each other. But these objects were dropped and rolled all over the floor. One was using balls, the other clubs. It should have been obvious to them that the balls and clubs did not mix.

'Funny thing!' said Trivia as they left the Hall of Economics. 'That always happens to me when I try. I thought they'd be better at it than me!'

o o o o o

As they walked down the road, they passed another small hall, from which they heard shouting within. A door opened and a Man Who Knows was pushed out. His clothing was dishevelled, his face was bruised, showing signs of blood; he looked as if he had been in a fight.

'Oh, I say!' exclaimed Snow, spontaneously.

'Look at that poor man – what ever's happened to him?' said Trivia.

Snow examined the daily programme of events. 'What's going on in there?' he asked. 'It says it ought to be a seminar on the *'Theory of Education'*.'

A Man Who Knows explained:

'They always have vigorous debates about education. Obviously his point of view was not accepted!'

Trivia spoke to the injured man: 'Are you all right? I shouldn't go back in there again'.

o o o o o

Jane Hyper-Byte was extraordinarily active as the Conference organiser, dashing from venue to venue in Knowhere to ensure that all the arrangements were working smoothly. Along the road, she rushed past Snow and Trivia, accompanied by an assistant pushing a trolley laden with thick computer print-outs. Hyper-Byte paused to give them each a copy.

'What's all this?' asked Snow.

'You'll need that as soon as possible,' answered Hyper-Byte, 'so that you can keep up to date with everything that is going on at the Conference. It's a record of the lectures in full and summaries of the seminars. All the information as events take place and it becomes available.'

'Not for me, thank you!' said Trivia. 'I just like to see what's happening.'

'There's tremendous efficiency,' commented Snow, as Hyper-Byte hurried off.

o o o o o

While walking in Knowhere, Snow and Trivia came upon the Man Who Knows from Off Shore. He was conspicuous enough in his holiday clothes, but his attitude was different, too. He was interesting to Snow, who was sensitive in his perceptions. He knew how to be tactful.

'You're enjoying yourself!' he said. 'You don't look as busy as the others.'

'No, I'm not,' replied this Man Who Knows. 'You see, I come from Off Shore'.

'Oh that's interesting – I suppose you will know all about finance, currencies, taxation and investment?'

'No I don't! You don't understand! I'm Off Shore – I'm not bothered with things like that. Other people do it for me.'

'Don't you ever come back into one of the big countries?' asked Trivia.

'Only for medical purposes. I've been back for a triple bypass operation on my heart and one hip replacement, so far.' As he spoke, he noticed an older, very distinguished-looking Man Who Knows walking past them. He went on:

'You see that man? He's the most senior one of us all! Every year he comes up with a brilliant lecture on all the latest moves in philosophy. He'll be speaking later on. He does a terrific job!'

'Will you go to hear him?' asked Snow.

'No!' he emphasised. 'No, I've been successful with Lady Luck. I don't want to get confused. You're doing all right, aren't you?' he said to Snow, while looking at Trivia.

'What are your interests that make you come here?' asked Trivia.

'My concerns are leisure and recreation, but those things don't stimulate them here. You see, where a lot of the guys come from, there's no call for it. But you watch them! By the end of the Conference, they won't be able to handle the situation! They become tense with all kinds of anxiety, they get stressed out, then complain they've got a headache and need to see a doctor! If you ask me, they should learn to relax, take some time off and enjoy themselves – that's what I do!'

o o o o o

Snow and Trivia were contemplating the seemingly casual ideas which pervaded life Off Shore, when a youthful Man Who Knows rushed up to them. He was in a state – hot, bothered and disconsolate. Trivia kindly asked him what was the matter.

'I'm lost,' he said, 'I'm lost! I'm looking for *'Meditation'*, the demonstration about meditation.'

Snow studied the programme on his clipboard. 'It's back where you've come from. Near here you could go to *'Yoga'*, *'Body Awareness'* or *'Chanting'*. Wouldn't they do, they're all quite soothing?'

'No! I wanted *'Meditation'*, said the youthful Man. 'The signposting makes me mad! I think I'll go back to my room and have a lie down.'

'Couldn't he do his meditation lying down?' asked Trivia, after he had gone.

o o o o o

Snow decided that he and Trivia should hear one of the major treatises being delivered, even though it would certainly be beyond their ability to understand it. He felt that they would absorb some benefit from the solemn atmosphere. His choice was: *'The Philosophical Application of Logic and Pure Mathematics to Physics, Music and Industry in the Twenty-first Century'*.

The most important lectures, like this one, were given in the Great Hall. The lecturer on this occasion was one of the oldest and most respected Men Who Know. As many of the younger Men Who Know as were available regarded it as a rare honour to be in the audience. Sitting dressed in their robes or gowns, they listened carefully to every word being spoken.

There was no other noise to be heard in the hall until the lecturer was nearly half way through. Then, faintly at first but growing louder, the sound of applause and cheering could be heard from outside. The Great Hall was situated on the main street of the town and had a balcony along its length overlooking it. As the noise of the cheering reached its loudest, all the younger men, practically the whole audience, rushed out on to the balcony. Snow wondered what they were going to see. A Man Who Knows told him:

'It's a celebrity! One of the greatest stars of the time is in town and passing by this afternoon. He makes a fortune – they all want to see him!'

'I'd like to see him too', said Trivia. 'Fancy them leaving the lecture for that!' The celebrity was driven along the street, receiving applause from the local population as well as many Men Who Know.

o o o o o

Snow and Trivia left the Great Hall, giving the rest of the lecture a miss. As they wandered on, Hyper-Byte came by with another stack of heavy documents.

'Ah,' she said, 'I must give you each a copy of this encyclopaedia! In one simple volume, we've collated and described all the recent innovations in communications technology, telling you how to use a modem on your telephone. You'll find it fascinating!'

Snow thanked Hyper-Byte politely saying that he would collect a copy later on. Trivia explained why she didn't want her copy:

'Thank you, but it won't be any use to me. My telephone is always engaged. I chatter away to my friends, our conversations are endless!'

'Well,' said Hyper-Byte, 'if we can't get through to you, you won't receive all the information to let you live properly.' She shrugged her shoulders and went on her way.

° ° ° ° °

In a small square an outdoor meeting was finishing. A Man Who Knows was concluding his address:

'Politicians agree that exports contribute enormously to improving a country's economy, a fact especially significant in a developing country. In the future, exports will be the life blood of each nation as global trade expands.' He concluded by thanking his listeners for their attention and asking if there were any questions.

The Men Who Know from the audience hurried off to their next assignments, so there was only one question – from Trivia:

'If all the nations trade together, will they all have one of those surpluses?'

'Trivia, don't ask that!' reprimanded Snow, pulling her away.

° ° ° ° °

There was one department which they had not yet visited, which was relevant to the purpose of Snow and Trivia at the Conference. It was the Department of Strategic and Tactical Analysis. It was here that the Men Who Know sought advice from each other, sometimes in debate, and sometimes through question and answer. They were always generous in sharing their skills among themselves. The visitors stayed for a while, enjoying the wisdom of the discussions.

'I get a lot of enquiries,' explained a junior Man, 'from young people wanting something new, something alternative, some kind of therapy. Would you advise me, I'm not certain what it's best to tell them?'

'There's many of these things around to choose from, cults, fashions, movements, ideas to believe in. It doesn't really matter what it is; it's just a thing to be occupied with temporarily. If you can believe in one, you can believe in another. Remember that people won't be young for very long. So find out what fad they're following now, then move them on to something else. Quickly they take in the new ideas and grow to like them. They'll be impressed by your knowledge and advice and grateful to you. Then the pressures of life overtake them and they forget all about it!'

Two Men Who Know disagreed with each other in the course of a debate.

'It's always best to give the citizens the advice they want to hear,' said the first. 'Mind you, quite often you have to establish in their minds what it is they will want to hear; otherwise they don't know!'

'I never give the people what they want!' responded the second. 'Firstly, they don't know what they want. Secondly, if you give them what they think they want, after a short while they won't like it anyway. No, you won't get anywhere giving people what they think they want. People are much better off, much happier, not knowing what they want!'

o o o o o

Towards the end of the Conference, Snow and Trivia

had sampled most of the activities, having a full record to describe to the Seekers. By the last evening there was only one place they had not been to – the Conference Bar. Primarily as a duty, though a pleasure too, it was appropriate that they should see the Men Who Know relaxing in a social setting.

The Conference Bar was surprisingly like so many others that Snow had patronized during his travels. The furnishings were of good quality in a nice style. It was comfortable. A few Men Who Know were sitting at the counter on bar stools; others sat on chairs in little groups round tables. A bartender served drinks. Some of the conversations were animated. Others were the desultory talk of tired men.

Snow and Trivia sat unobtrusively at a side table. They ordered drinks from the steward and watched the proceedings. They could not help overhearing conversations between Men Who Know.

Two old friends were catching up on each other's news.

'Did you have a good year – any memorable features?'

'The main event was that I bought a new car.'

'I remember you telling me you liked cars, but I thought you had a very good one.'

'Yes, but I needed a bigger one for the family. My wife gave birth to more offspring.'

'Oh that's wonderful – a boy or a girl?'

'Both! She had twins. Well, what can you do? Even in our profession, you can't plan such things. The main thing is that I got a decent new car out of it. I chose the colour blue.'

Trivia was unsettled by what she took to be the order of priorities of this Man Who Knows. She asked Snow if the man really rated a blue car as being more important than his new baby children. Snow too was mystified, but he pointed out that many men in high positions, even rulers, still loved their cars.

o o o o o

Trivia listened to another conversation and was amazed to hear that it was about – football! A small group was holding an intense, animated argument.

'Do you still support your home club?'

'Certainly! I see all the home games but I'm too busy to travel away with the team.'

'Why did they sack your manager? Bit of a mistake, wasn't it?'

'Well, he should never have sold the youngster. He got a good price, but the money isn't everything. He was a goalscorer, and no matter how good the rest of the team, you must have a player to score goals. Like the rest of life, if you don't get goals, you don't score!'

Once more Trivia was taken by surprise. She had never expected such distinguished clever men like these to be concerned with a mere game. But Snow informed her that there were usually some philosophers and other learned spectators in the crowd at a top-class match.

o o o o o

'Did you see the celebrity, the star go by?' whispered a Man Who Knows to his neighbour. 'They make some money, don't they? They say he's a millionaire several times over! He has two bodyguards.'

'I hear that our senior man was brilliant as usual in his latest lecture on philosophy. It's a miracle that he can be both so intelligible and knowledgeable at the same time.'

'Did you hear his talk?'

'No, I didn't actually go myself! I shall read it up later.'

o o o o o

Halfway through the evening, the Man Who Knows from Off Shore strode into the Bar. Just inside the door was a discreet receptacle for litter into which he threw all the Conference papers he had been carrying. He caught sight of the senior Man Who Knows. Naturally it was polite that he should exchange a few words with him.

'All the talk among the Men Who Know here is about your lecture on the trends in philosophy – the star piece of the whole Conference! It was brilliant, they say....'

'Oh, oh, really? I'm surprised they're saying that. Because – nobody came! Not one!'

'Oh, I am sorry – that's awful! For me it was my last chance to see a film, a thriller. That's why I missed it, but I sure look forward to reading it.'

'Don't worry about it, my friend,' said the older man. 'The same thing happens every year. I'm used to it.'

The bartender was observant. He noticed that the Man Who Knows from Off Shore, one of his best patrons, had committed an embarrassing faux pas. He hurried across to see if a calming drink would help to restore serenity.

'Yes, Sir, thank you. I'll take a Black Volcano!' was the reply from the Off Shore Man.

o o o o o

At the end of the evening, Snow remarked to Trivia that the Men Who Know didn't spend all their time discussing serious issues. 'No, they don't,' said Trivia. 'A lot of it is a bit like the gossip I listen to back at the Roundabout. I think I could almost join in, although they're supposed to be much cleverer than I am.'

Snow advised caution. 'I shouldn't try that. I guess that, at the end of the day, they have to take it easy like ordinary people.'

The visitors left the Bar while it was still crowded. The stamina for socialising displayed by some of those present was remarkable.

o o o o o

There was energy enough to maintain the momentum of the Conference right up until its close. When that time was reached, Snow had the impression of two strong feelings. Firstly, as there was finally no more work to be done, the energy gave way to a sense of tiredness. Secondly, over-riding the first sensation, there was exhilaration and immense satisfaction in completing the programme, a joy and a thrill that so much had been achieved in a short time, largely because of the sustained pressure.

The Conference ended where it had begun, with a ceremony in the Great Hall. The unity of the Men Who Know had been enhanced by the sharing of hard work together and the deepening of both old and new friendships. The benign camaraderie of the assembly was unmistakeable

Jane Hyper-Byte had the honour of giving the closing address:

'This has been, I think, the most fruitful Conference

I can remember. The depth and seriousness of the discussions, the breadth of imagination, the width of experience, the understanding, the sensitivity, the co-operation and collaboration, the concentration of effort – all these attributes have been evident in producing levels of excellence seldom achieved and which will be so beneficial to those whom we serve. I offer my congratulations to you all for lasting out through a strenuous round of events. You go off now with my greatest good wishes for the year ahead.'

After some whole-hearted applause, the playing of the organ was heard for a final song. The Men Who Know, all dressed in their robes and gowns, anticipated the moment and rose to their feet eagerly to sing with their friends:

'We must remain in the ascendancy,
Dominant, sovereign in the ascendancy,
Never obscure, never unsure,
Always upright in our answers.

'When we have answered all their questions,
We know that they will not agree among themselves,
Whatever we say, anyway,
Which helps us to remain in the ascendancy.

'Sometimes they try something else for a little while,
But it never lasts for very long.
And then they eventually return to us
Because we are in the ascendancy.

'We must remain in the ascendancy,
Dominant, sovereign in the ascendancy,
Stand by what's right, speak out and fight,
For duty, honour and truth,
For duty, honour and truth.'

At the end of the Conference, Snow and Trivia were busy saying good-bye and exchanging good wishes with the many fine friends they had met. At last their own special Man Who Knows, the one who had invited them, emerged from the throng to greet them:

'Hasn't it all been tremendous?' he said. 'The benefits and advantages one gets from attending a Conference like this are overwhelming. How did you get on? Did you find your way around all right?'

'It's all been very interesting, Sir; thank you so much for inviting us to be observers. I've not seen anything like it before.' Snow answered with his customary good manners. It was not possible to tell whether or not he was hiding some scepticism.

Trivia's response was also in keeping with her character: 'I loved seeing all the various Men,' she said openly. 'A lot of different sorts.'

'Now let me take you back to meet your companions again,' said the Man Who Knows, as he led them off to the green where they had first seen him.

7

Aftermath

It depends what you mean by wisdom,
For it's not always easy to see — *Trivia*

THE SEEKERS were sitting about casually on the green, some on benches and others on the grass. Woody had asked Jaz to keep an eye out for the return of Snow and Trivia, thinking rather pompously that it would give the young man something to occupy his attention constructively. But as Woody saw the two of them approaching, accompanied by the Man Who Knows, he noted that Jaz had let him down in that little task.

'I've had to do it myself,' he moaned. 'It's always the way, but it's best to do things yourself.'

Molly, having more compassion, corrected him: 'That's a boring thing for Jaz to do! You shouldn't expect a boy to have such patience.'

If there was a touch of friction within the group, it was caused by all the waiting. When the whole party was gathered together again, every one of the Seekers had questions to ask, as if in urgent cross-examination.

'I can't wait to hear about it,' said Helen.

'Good morning, Mr Snow.' There was envy in Woody's voice. 'How are you? Those of us who were not granted the privileges which you have received would like to hear a full report.'

'Please describe it all to us,' added Growth with his intellectual curiosity.

'Did they know all about football?' bawled Jaz. 'Did they know who's going to win the World Cup?'

'Jaz, they knew all about everything, including football,' said Trivia tenderly.

Molly in her maturity was more restrained in her desire for information:

'We are a bit impatient, as you can see. Knowhere is a marvellous place, it's been nice to be able to see it. All the people we met have been so friendly. But the trouble is that all the time we were thinking of you, wondering what you were seeing?'

'We've all had guesses about what you were up to,' confirmed Debbie.

Woody could no longer contain himself. 'Now, please Snow, will you tell us all about it, what happens there? I want to know if I can have any hopes of participating myself one day.'

'Of course, I'll tell you,' began Snow. 'It was as entertaining an experience as I've ever had. I think, Woody, you would have approved of the organisation. The procedures were carried out with meticulous precision. The style, the refinement, the knowledge, the expertise, the skills, the imagination, the inventiveness, the power of thought, the diversity of experience, all were displayed to an unparalleled degree of excellence. Altogether it was most unusual!'

Rupert as always wanted to focus on the things that mattered to him. 'Could you be more precise? I want to hear about the details.'

The Man Who Knows sensed that Rupert might be difficult for Snow to deal with, so he thought it might be helpful if he answered that question.

'All the Men Who Know are there,' he said. 'They have to come to this annual convention to keep their learning abreast of current developments and advances.'

Snow then described to the Seekers how the Conference worked. He told them about Jane Hyper-Byte, young, bright and brilliant, who organised every aspect from beginning to end, so that nothing went wrong. He astonished them, even Growth, by describing the variety and range of subjects and disciplines that were covered. He reminded them, as he had pointed out to Trivia, that these were trained men in their calling, specialists, who were able to master all the tricks of their trade.

Rupert was not satisfied. He was irritated by the evasion.

'I'd like to have more details.' Rupert's voice was louder. 'For example, what did you and Trivia actually do? Did you attend all the lectures? Do you mean to say that Trivia is now an expert in all those subjects?'

Trivia answered for herself: 'It's funny, you know, but I did actually think that I could hold a conversation with these clever men, although my sort of ideas is different from theirs.'

Snow confessed that they had not attended all the lectures. They had considered it best to get a broad picture of the choice of options. In any case, all the information was published comprehensively and could therefore be read at one's convenience.

Rupert was angry. Delay in coming to the point was alien to the sort of man he had made himself.

'Look,' he exclaimed, 'could we possibly get down to business?'

Rupert dispensed with Snow and addressed the Man Who Knows. 'In order for my corporations to thrive, by which I mean make profits on a rising scale, I must know the trends, so that I can make detailed predictions for years ahead. Now, come on, did you meet the right Man to help me?'

The Man Who Knows retained his composure. 'The Conference doesn't work like that. Matters are dealt with in a general way. It is the big issues that are examined. It is not the place to learn an answer for a particular individual. That is an unreasonable expectation!'

Rupert was even more exasperated: 'I know all about the big issues,' he snarled rudely. 'The ideas I have already are perfectly sound. I'm looking for advice to improve my business prospects. Can you outline the logical steps in front of me? You can't tell me, can you?'

Snow tried to calm the situation by telling Rupert that he should work at it by himself – like the Men Who Know do.

Taking up that point, Helen declared that she had worked hard by herself all her life. Through these efforts, she now felt she had reached a position from which she ought to shoot forward. She needed accurate advice telling her how to progress to a new status.

Snow told her about the brilliant lecture on philosophy. He offered to lend her his copy of it so that she could read it. That would help her make up her mind.

'I'm much too busy to do a lot more reading,' protested Helen. 'Isn't there someone who's done all that, who can be ready with some answers? I assumed that would be a Man Who Knows.'

'Well, if there is, we didn't see him.' Snow had to disappoint her. 'Remember, the Conference lectures are thorough. You can rely on the accuracy of the general philosophic principles and apply them to yourself.'

I really don't know what I've come all this way for, thought Helen. She wondered whether the Men Who Know really were professionals.

Despite Rupert's anger and Helen's resignation, Growth was optimistic that his own journey was not a wild-goose chase.

'Did you meet any economic experts?' he asked. 'The economy is such a huge topic nowadays. I expect they give a lot of time to it, using the best brains available.'

'Yes, we saw some of them,' answered Trivia, remembering all the jugglers she had watched. 'They were sweet and tried so hard, but they just couldn't agree between themselves! They got so upset. But the trouble, it looked to me, was that they blamed each other for the disagreements.'

Growth did not value Trivia's opinion about economics. So he asked another question in his optimism:

'Do you think they could help me formulate a new theory?' he said.

'No, I shouldn't think so for a moment,' Trivia replied, adamantly. Trying to be kind, she went on, 'If you want my advice, I should carry on by yourself; it will be much better for you.'

Debbie had loved the friendships of the journey and felt at home in the friendliness of Knowhere. She was in good heart as she sought the clarifications that would help her. She asked Snow:

'Did they know anything about new perceptions and aspirations, or did they just stick to the old ambitions? We can only contribute to our communities properly, be really satisfied, when we understand ourselves fully. Did they deal with this?'

'Of course; very much so,' Snow assured her.

'You can have as much hypnosis and massage as you like!' interjected Trivia, but it wasn't a very helpful remark.

'Trivia, this is a serious subject,' warned Snow. 'The senior Men Who Know pass on the benefit of all their experience to the younger men for the future.'

Debbie was still not clear in her mind. 'I feel a bit muddled and uncertain,' she said, 'because I have been on several courses and tried all sorts of remedies recommended by friends, but nothing yet has produced the answer for me. It shouldn't be too difficult for an expert, should it?'

'The Men Who Know are aware,' Snow informed her, 'of everything that is available. I think they would say to you, 'Keep trying, there's bound to be a therapy that suits you, if you can find it."

Molly was delighted to hear that younger men were being taught by their respected seniors. It was a safeguard for the future. As she said: 'Perhaps it is surprising at my age, but I am concerned with the future, what is to come for my grandchildren. Changes, changes, changes, that's all there's been throughout my life, and not all of them for the good. When will the future come? Is it here? Are we there yet?'

'Cheer up, Molly,' advised Trivia. 'Don't worry about that. I don't think about it at all. I suppose if the future's going to come, come it will. We can deal with that later. We can't deal with it now, can we?'

Molly looked sadly at the Man Who Knows. It was the first time the Seekers had seen her down-hearted and yielding to her age.

'This is my last chance,' she pleaded. 'Is there no-one who can help me, not even in Knowhere?'

'I'm sorry,' responded the Man Who Knows, 'I'm truly, very sorry. I'm sorry.' He began to walk away. He had been moved by the sincerity of the plea of the grandmother and had felt obliged to admit that he knew not how to help her.

The Seekers were stunned by this admission. It was also a setback for themselves. But Snow was always generous and magnanimous. The Man Who Knows had become a kind friend and so Snow brought him back into the group.

Woody was insensitive to the delicate change of attitude in the party. He wondered if Snow and Trivia had been able to meet the Men Who Know off duty.

'Oh yes,' said Snow, 'we were able to meet some of them for a drink and a chat in the bar.'

Helen was amazed; it would never have occurred to her to take a drink while on duty at work. Woody enlightened them all by citing his own experience that everyone in authority needed to relax and relieve the pressure after a hard day's work.

'They were quite nice,' said Trivia, 'when you got to know them over a drink. The Conference as a whole was not a bundle of fun – but we had some fun with them in the bar, didn't we, Snow?'

'Well,' said Molly, 'if they all spend time each day drinking in a bar, no wonder they can't answer our questions! Reasonable questions at that.'

'I've come all this way to be told to carry on doing what I was doing already,' repeated Helen.

Rupert was always conscious of the expenditure of time, whether or not it had been profitably used. He realised that not one Seeker had received satisfactory answers.

'We're all in the same boat,' he indicated. 'We do have some companionship, which we didn't have before. That's something I suppose, but it's not money.'

Debbie spoke of different values. 'I love friendships. I've always had lots of friends. Because of our journey together, I feel I've got some new ones, even if I haven't got the answers I came for.'

It was not possible for Jaz at his age to understand the thoughts of the adults. To him it was dismaying that they did not seem to be as happy with the outcome of the venture as he was.

He voiced his displeasure: 'If all you grown-ups can't get what you want, why bother about it? Why bother with knowledge or wisdom?'

'I've been thinking,' said Growth. 'I bet that, truthfully, after our journey to arrive in Knowhere, we are just as wise, know just as much as the Men Who Know anyway. Not one of our questions has been answered. Not by them! But somehow it doesn't seem to matter any more.'

'Time marches on,' said Molly, 'but wisdom stays the same. Elusive as ever. You continually need new people to understand and represent it. I'm not going to think about it. I have enjoyed the journey with you all enormously. I've been very lucky. Thank you!'

'We *all* seem to be People Who Know,' said Jaz.

'Yes, that's it,' agreed Helen, 'that can be my new status. Let's call ourselves *'The People Who Know'*.'

o o o o o

The adventure was over. The Seekers returned to the daily routines that they knew so well. They said their farewells to each other, moved by the varying degrees of affection which were their habit. There was no sadness. There were no regrets. They had all enjoyed themselves. They all felt they had learned something which would be helpful to them, though if called upon, they would each have defined what it was in a different way.

Before the Seekers split up to go their separate ways, Snow composed a tune and wrote a song for them:

'Into the future, we go
Into the future.
Will I belong, when the road takes another turn,
Now that I realise no one man
Knows the mystery of the way?

'Will you come along, walk with me for a while?
Troubles may come and go, but together we'll
move on.

'What I know to-day
May not be to-morrow's world,
And chance plays a greater part,
So I must wait for what destiny may bring.

'Will you come along, walk with me for a while?
Together we'll look to the sun,
Be ready for another day.

'Into the future, we go
Into the future.'

When he wrote this song, Snow was thinking of Trivia, but the Seekers didn't realise that.

Trivia was pondering over all the things that had happened since she first met the Seekers at the Roundabout. On reflection, she thought how surprising it was that they had been seeking answers from a Man Who Knows.

'Do you think that they were looking in the right place?' asked Trivia.

'I doubt it,' replied Snow.

THE END